Blade

by

Chris Powling

Illustrated by Alan Marks

First published in 2005 in Great Britain by
Barrington Stoke Ltd
18 Walker Street, Edinburgh, EH3 7LP

www.barringtonstoke.co.uk

Reprinted 2006, 2008, 2010

ISBN: 978-1-84299-338-5

Printed in Great Britain by Bell & Bain Ltd

A Note from the Author

A lot of this story is true. Years ago, I really did meet a kid like Toxon. And he really did have a knife like Blade. Today, though, I'd tell a grown-up as soon as I could. That way, none of us need have any nightmares.

For Jake
... but only when he's old enough

Contents

Chapter 1
Bad Dream

Think Hitler.

Think Stalin.

Think Saddam Hussein.

Now mix them together. That's how I felt about Toxon when I was your age. OK, I know this sounds over the top. What kind of a kid is so scary he reminds you of monsters like these? Toxon, that's who.

I only met him twice – more than 40 years ago. Yet I still dream about him. I see him standing in front of me. He looks large as life and twice as ugly. I wake up shivering and dripping with sweat. I don't dare go back to sleep in case he's still there.

So think terror, right? Think Toxon.

Chapter 2
New Kids

It was our first day at Upper School.

Even my mad mate Lee wasn't too happy.

"Just look at us, Rich," he grumbled.
"New blazers, new shoes, new school-bag.
I feel a right dummy."

"That's why the older kids can always spot us," I said. "You've even got a new eye-patch, Lee!"

"My mum made it," Lee said.

Lee had been born with only one eye. His right eye was perfect – the same as yours or mine. His left eye was just a lump. It looked like a peeled grape. He used to scare the little kids at our last school by lifting his pink eye-patch. Then he wobbled the lump at them. They ran off yelling, you can bet.

Not any more, though. "You're at Upper School now," I said. "No tricks like that at this place."

"No little kids here either," said Lee.

"Only us, of course."

"Yeah, Rich ... only us."

We took a careful look round the yard. It was very grey and stony at Upper School. There were stone steps, stone walls, stone

passages. Even the doors and windows had a grey and stony look.

So did the faces of the big kids – those who looked at us at all.

One of them drifted our way.

"You new kids?" he asked.

"Yes ..."

"Shall I tell you something, then?"

"If you like."

"Stay away from Toxon, OK?"

"Toxon?" I said.

"Who's Toxon?" Lee asked.

The big kid stared at us as if we came from another planet.

"You don't know who Toxon is?"

"No, I don't," I said.

"Nor do I," said Lee.

"You'd better find out fast then," the big kid laughed. "Before Toxon finds out about you ..."

Chapter 3
Blade

It wasn't just us. It was the same for every kid who wore a smart blazer. Every so often, an older kid would come up and tap you on the back. "You new here?" he'd say.

"Yeah ... how can you tell?"

"Met Toxon yet?"

"Not yet, no ..."

"*Just stay away from him, OK?*"

They told us stories, too. About the party games Toxon used to play. Also about something he called "Blade".

"Party games?" Lee said. "And who's this 'Blade', Rich?"

"It's a knife," I told him.

"A knife?"

"I think so," I said. "Don't ask me what kind though. I just heard about it somewhere."

"A *Blade*," said Lee, making a face.

I didn't like the word, either. It had a cold, steely ring to it. It made me keener than ever to keep clear of Toxon.

How hard could that be, anyway? After all, Upper School wasn't just grey and stony. It was huge as well. There were about 1,000 kids in all to hide Lee and me from Toxon.

Then I made my big mistake.

Chapter 4
Short Cut

I did something very, very stupid.
I should never have taken the short cut
behind the gym.

But I'm late for the lesson, I told myself.
Anyway, who's going to see me?

At first, I thought I'd got away with it.
The short cut was just what you'd expect at
Upper School. It was a grey, stony outside
passage dotted with thorn bushes. Then,
when I was halfway along, one of the
bushes moved. "Come here, new kid,"
growled a voice.

I knew at once who it was.

To his right was a tall, beefy minder. To
his left was another minder – even more
tall and beefy. Don't ask me to say what
the kid in the middle looked like. Just think

of something hard, and greasy, that skulks in dark corners. He crooked a finger to bring me closer. "Know who I am, new kid?" he asked.

"Toxon," I said.

"The very person," he said. "And this happens to be my patch. What are you doing on my patch, new kid?"

"Your patch?"

"The patch you're standing on," said Toxon.

"I didn't know that," I gulped. "Honest, I didn't. I'm sorry, Toxon. Shall I go right now?"

"Go right now? I'm afraid it's not as simple as that. We've still got to sort out a little matter of payment, payment for invading my patch."

"But I haven't got any money!"

"No money? In that case ... let's have your hymn book."

"My hymn book?"

"It's in the top pocket of your blazer. With your name inside it. It's a school rule, new kid. You have to have it, so the masters can find out who you are."

I put my hand in my pocket. "Here it is ..."

Toxon grinned as he took the hymn book. On either side of him, his two minders shuffled their feet. They knew what was coming next.

"Thanks, new kid," Toxon sniffed. "Now then ... are you ready for a little party game?"

Chapter 5
The Game

Toxon flicked through my hymn book.
In the shadow of the thorn bush, he looked
old and toad-like. I couldn't take my eyes
off him. "You a good reader, new kid?" he
asked.

"Pretty good," I said.

"Can you read a hymn ... without any mistakes?"

"I think so."

"Good," he said. "Very good. Because that's what you've got to do in this party game of mine. It goes like this. I choose a hymn and you read it out loud ... without making a mistake. Are you with me so far?"

"What ... what if I do make a mistake?"

"Good question," said Toxon.

He slid his hand inside his blazer. "I'm glad you asked me that, new kid," he went on. "You'll like the next bit. You see, for every mistake you make you get a kiss."

"A kiss?"

"Yes, a kiss ... from my little friend."

I looked at him, blankly. What little friend? Then he took his hand out of his blazer. He was holding the handle of a

knife. Just the handle, that's all – a plain, flat handle about as long as a pencil. "This is my little friend, new kid," Toxon said. "And here's how she gives you a kiss …"

He pressed the knife handle.

At once, something thin and sharp and nasty sprang out of it. The knife was as long as two pencils now. Toxon bent forward with a silky smile. "What do you think of my little friend, new kid?" he asked. "I call her 'Blade'."

"Blade," I said softly.

"Well done, new kid! You know what?
I think Blade's taken a real fancy to you. I
can see she's *longing* to give you a kiss. So
why don't we start the game?"

Again, he pressed the knife.

The blade flicked back into the handle.
Toxon held it between his finger and
thumb. Now, the handle was level with my
eye. It was exactly a pencil's length away.
He opened the hymn book with his other

hand. "Read this one," he said. "And no mistakes, OK?"

I still thought I could do it. I'd been singing hymns in school assembly for years. I mustn't panic, that was the important thing – just keep my gaze on the printed page.

Then Toxon did something I'll never forget. It was every bit as scary as my first glimpse of Blade.

He turned my hymn book upside down.

"Go ahead, new kid," he hissed. "Read it now."

Chapter 6
Lee

At first, I was too scared to tell anyone.
It took Lee a week to find out what was
wrong with me. When at last I told him
what had happened, his face went white.
"Upside down?" he said. "Toxon made you
read the hymn upside down?"

"Every word," I said.

"How did you do it, Rich?"

"I got lucky, that's all. He'd chosen a hymn I knew off-by-heart. We often sang it at our last school. I didn't need the hymn book at all. I just let Toxon *think* I was reading."

"So you didn't make any mistakes ..." said Lee.

"Not one," I choked. "Not even with Blade ready to kiss me at any moment."

I'd started to shake again. I may have been crying as well. OK, so this wasn't very brave for a 13-year-old. I didn't care any more – not after all those bad dreams.

Lee was hugging me now. I could feel him shaking, too. This wasn't from fear, though. In his case, it was anger. "He's sick," he snapped. "This Toxon kid is sick. He wants the whole school to be scared of him."

"It already is, Lee."

"Well, he's got to be stopped. If he isn't, we'll have another Hitler on our hands one day."

"Or another Stalin," I added.

"Besides," Lee said, "I bet he's bluffing."

"Bluffing?"

"He's all talk, I reckon. Most bullies are like that. Toxon would crumble if you stood up to him."

"Oh yeah?" I said. "Suppose he isn't like most bullies, though? Suppose he's the kind that won't crumble?"

"Somebody's got to take that risk, Rich."

"Like who?"

Lee stared into space. His face was still white with anger. Somehow, this made his

eye-patch seem pinker than ever. He was

in one of his mad moods, I could tell. It was

the sort of mood when anything could

happen. "Maybe it's got to be me," he said.

Chapter 7
Eye to Eye

Next day, we bunked off lessons. I bet this was the first time ever for a couple of new kids at Upper School. So I was scared twice over as we slipped into the passage behind the gym.

Toxon was standing there in the shadows. His minders were just behind him – looking bigger than ever to me.

Toxon's eyes turned to slits when he saw us. He spat on the ground in disgust. "Well, stack me," he said, wiping his mouth. "If it isn't a pair of new kids! I've met one of them before, I think. But not the one with the eye-patch ..."

Lee jogged me with his elbow. "Hey, Rich," he asked, "which of these kids is Toxon?"

"Him," I pointed.

"Him?" Lee frowned. "You mean the small one?"

Toxon's sneer froze on his face.
"A joker, eh?" he said, softly. "I like kids who can joke. So does my little friend. She sorts them out with a kiss, you know ... real quick."

"Really?" said Lee. "So where is this little friend?"

"Here," said Toxon.

The knife glinted in the air. As he pressed its handle, the blade flicked in-and-out, in-and-out, in-and-out. It looked as if tiny flashes of light were trapped in his fist. Lee gave a yawn. "Oh, that little friend," he said. "I remember now – the one you poke in kids' faces. I suppose you think it's scary."

"Don't you think so, new kid?"

"Not much."

Lee lifted his hand as if he were holding a knife himself. You couldn't see it really, of course. He was only acting. But you could see it in your mind.

We watched Lee flick this unseen knife in-and-out, in-and-out, in-and-out – just a pencil's length away from his eye. "Now that's what I call scary," he said. "When you poke a blade in your own face."

"In your *own* face?"

"As near as you dare," Lee said. "It takes a lot more guts than reading hymns."

"You think so?"

"Hey! This could be our party game, Toxon! We could play it right now. You against me. The winner is the one who gets the blade closest to his eye. We have one go each, OK? These big guys will do the judging. What do you think?"

Toxon licked his lips. "I think it's a con, new kid. You've got con-man written all over you. You against me? Here on my

patch? You'd never take that kind of risk ..."

"Wouldn't I?" said Lee. "I've done it

before, you know!"

"You've done it before?"

"Look, I'll show you."

Coolly, Lee lifted his eye-patch. Of

course, his lump wasn't new to me. It still

made me think of a peeled grape, though.

Toxon stared at it in horror. His mouth slowly sagged open. "You did that to yourself?" he said. "With a knife?"

"Well, you're bound to get it wrong a few times," Lee said. "Knives can be really tricky to work with. Shall we start the game, Toxon? I'll go first if you like."

"You're a nutter," Toxon spat.

He turned to his minders. "He's a nutter, right? What kind of kid even thinks of a game like that?"

The bigger, beefier minder gave a shrug. "OK, so he's a nutter," he said. "What difference does that make? He's still on your patch, isn't he? Are you taking him on or not?"

"Make up your mind," said his mate.

"But that's stupid! One slip of the knife and I'd end up—"

"Like him?"

We all stared at Lee. His good eye was gleaming madly. Was it this that showed Toxon he was serious? Was he really so keen to start the game?

The lump in his bad eye wobbled.

"Ready when you are, Tox," said my best mate.

Toxon shook his head. "Got better things to do with my time," he gulped. "Coming, you two?"

The minders took a good long look at him. Then, both of them laughed. "Not yet, Tox," said one.

"If ever, Tox," said the other.

"But this kid is—"

"Tox," said the bigger one. "It's over, OK?"

They didn't bother to watch Toxon leave his patch. Nor did they move off themselves till he was well out of sight. That's when the bigger one gave Lee a wink. "Nice one, nutter," he said.

Chapter 8
Goodbye, Blade

That was the last I ever saw of Toxon – except, of course, in my dreams. Some kids said he was sent to another school. Others told us he left at the end of term to get a job. "Who cares, anyway?" I said to Lee. "As long as he took Blade with him."

"He didn't," Lee said. "I found it under the thorn bush the day after. He must have dropped it."

"So where is it now?"

"I broke it up and dumped the bits in a bin."

Trust Lee to finish the job. Trust him not to show off about it, too. A hero is like that. Mind you, I'm glad times have changed in the last 40 years. Schools today have got bullies sussed. Always tell a grown-up, that's the best thing. That way, everyone gets the help they need – even the bully.

Remember, I simply got lucky years ago. We can't all be best mates with a mad kid who wears an eye-patch.

Barrington Stoke would like to thank all its readers for commenting on the manuscript before publication and in particular:

E. Armstrong
Lucy Barnsby
Emma Chapman
Jane Cooper
David Gardner
Phillip Iley
Nathan Potts
N. Nees
Haydon Smith

Become a Consultant!

Would you like to be a consultant? Ask your parent, carer or teacher to contact us at the email address below – we'd love to hear from them! They can also find out more by visiting our website.

schools@barringtonstoke.co.uk
www.barringtonstoke.co.uk